The art in this book was painted with watercolor and gouache on lanaquarelle paper.

Morgan Plays Soccer Text copyright © 2001 by Anne Rockwell
Illustrations copyright © 2001 by Paul Meisel Printed in the U.S.A. All rights reserved. www.harperchildrens.com

Library of Congress Cataloging-in-Publication Data
Rockwell, Anne F.
  Morgan plays soccer / by Anne Rockwell ; illustrated by Paul Meisel.
    p.   cm.
  Summary: Morgan Brownbear has trouble playing soccer until his coach, Mr. Monkey, finds the perfect position for him.
  ISBN 0-06-028440-4. — ISBN 0-06-028444-7 (lib. bdg.)
  [1. Soccer—Fiction.   2. Bears—Fiction.   3. Animals—Fiction.]   I. Meisel, Paul, ill.   II. Title.
PZ7.R5943Mp   2001
[E]—dc21   99-39894
                                                                                                                CIP

Typography by Matt Adamec   1 2 3 4 5 6 7 8 9 10   ❖   First Edition

MORGAN PLAYS SOCCER

BY **ANNE ROCKWELL**
ILLUSTRATED BY **PAUL MEISEL**

HARPERCOLLINSPUBLISHERS

TO: Morgan
Brownbear

The day Morgan Brownbear moved

to a new house in a new neighborhood,

a package arrived. It was a present

from his aunt Lucy—a great-looking,

silky, ultra-blue violet shirt with a big

white number one printed on the back.

Morgan put it on and went outside.

His neighbor Nina Jane Monkey

was kicking a ball. "What position do

you play?" she asked him.

"What do you mean?" said Morgan.

"I mean that since you're wearing

a soccer jersey, you must play soccer.

Don't you?" asked Nina Jane.

Morgan shook his head.

"Never mind. Let's go over to

my house," said Nina Jane.

After he saw her room, Morgan understood how
much Nina Jane loved soccer. She even convinced
Morgan he wanted to play, too.

Morgan's father took him to the sporting goods store to buy the equipment he needed. He got new shorts, shin guards, long socks, and cleats.

On Saturday morning Morgan

couldn't wait to put on his soccer

clothes.

When he got to the park, lots of other players had come.

Nina Jane's father, Mr. Monkey, was the coach.

He showed everyone how to stretch and warm up

by running around the field four times.

Then Mr. Monkey blew his whistle. "Okay, everybody!" he said. "Listen up. In soccer you try to get the ball to a goal and score a point for your team. The rules are: You're allowed to kick the ball—like this. You're allowed to dribble the ball—like this. Later on you'll learn to head the ball—like this. But don't catch it with your hands!"

Everyone was extremely eager to start.

Mr. Monkey said, "Okay—today we're going to start by practicing kicking and dribbling. If I blow my whistle, stop and listen to what I have to say!"

Morgan was pretty good at kicking. He was able to kick the ball across the field in one hard kick, just like Nina Jane.

When Mr. Monkey said it was time to practice dribbling,
Morgan tried to dribble the way Mr. Monkey did. He put
the ball between his feet and tried to push it from one foot
to the other, always moving it forward. But he just couldn't
seem to do it. He kept tripping over the ball.

"Time to practice dribbling and passing," said Mr. Monkey. Katie Catz kicked the ball to Morgan. Morgan grabbed it and ran all the way across the field. He was so proud of himself, he didn't notice that Mr. Monkey was blowing the whistle loudly.

"Remember what I told you, everyone!"

Mr. Monkey called. "Kick the ball! Dribble it!

But don't carry it in your hands!"

Morgan was so embarrassed! After soccer practice he said to Nina Jane, "I don't want to play soccer anymore. I'm no good at it."

"You just need to work on your drills," she said. "I'll help you practice, if you like."

Morgan shook his head. "No, thanks. Playing soccer is too hard."

But Nina Jane wouldn't give up. She kept after Morgan until he agreed to let her coach him. Every day she showed Morgan how to kick the ball with a pointed toe. She showed him how to dribble it up and down the yard without tripping over it once. Every day Morgan got better and better.

On Saturday morning Mr. Monkey divided everyone into

teams. He gave each player a "Purple Hardware Parakeets"

or "Cobb's Supermarket Canaries" soccer jersey.

Nina Jane's was purple. Morgan's was yellow.

"Nina Jane! We're not on the same team," Morgan wailed.

"It's okay," she said. "You'll be fine. And just because we're on different teams, that doesn't mean we can't still be friends."

As soon as everyone was on the field, Mr. Monkey said, "First we're going to have a scrimmage. That's a practice game. Then we're going to keep score."

When the scrimmage began, Morgan forgot everything

he had learned. He became so excited, he caught the ball

in both hands.

Mr. Monkey blew the whistle. Morgan had never felt so humiliated.

Mr. Monkey walked over to him. "Morgan, you're very good at catching a ball with your hands. But that's against the rules—unless you're a goalie. The goalie's job is to keep the ball out of his goal. Would you like to be your team's goalie?"

"Me?" asked Morgan nervously.

Mr. Monkey smiled. "Yes, you. You'll do just fine."

As Morgan put on his goalie shirt

and gloves, he worried.

What if he did something wrong?

What if he let his whole team down?

As he stood in front of the goal,

Morgan felt scared and lonely.

Then Nina Jane kicked the ball across the field. It came whizzing through the air.

Morgan leaped and caught it in his hands. He heard a loud noise. This time it wasn't Mr. Monkey blowing his whistle.

It was the sound of cheering.

"Great save, Morgan!" yelled Nina Jane.

It was true. Morgan had kept that great kick from going

into the goal. It was a great save.

And that day he did it again and again.

To Nicholas and Christian
—A.R.

For Joe, Diane,
Joey, and Andrew
—P.M.

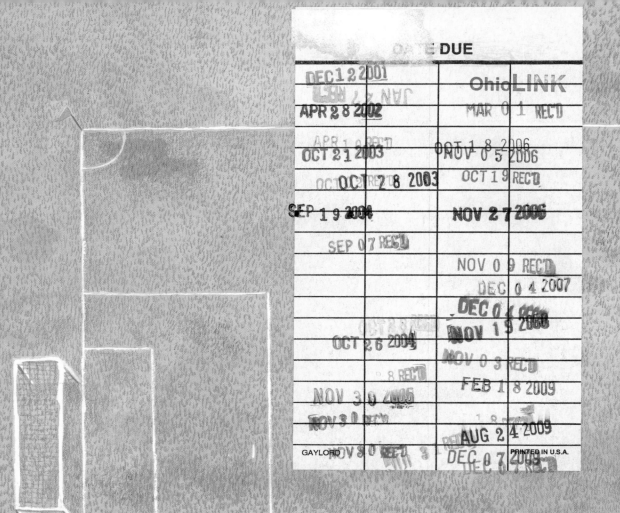